LAWRENCE PUBLIC LIBRARY

3 1549 00311 822 0

O9-AIE-225

3/02

SO. LAWRENCE BRANCH LIBRARY
135 Parker St.
Lawrence, MA   01843

LAWRENCE PUBLIC
LIBRARY
South Lawrence Branch

135 Parker Street
Lawrence, Massachusetts
794-5789

Established 1927

SPACE GUYS!

Martha Weston

beep....beep....beep....

Holiday House/New York

For Bill and Allison—
studio mates and pals for life

Copyright © 2000 by Martha Weston
All Rights Reserved
Printed in the United States of America
First Edition

Library of Congress Cataloging-in-Publication Data
Weston, Martha.
Space guys! / Martha Weston.—1st ed.
   p.   cm.
Summary: A boy is visited by beings that look like robots that arrive in a
flying saucer from outer space.
ISBN 0-8234-1487-6
[1. Extraterrestrial beings Fiction. 2. Stories in rhyme.]
I. Title.
PZ8.3.W4999Sp 2000
[E]—dc21   99-34267
CIP

Reading Level: 1.3

beep....beep....beep....

Beep! Beep!
No sleep.
I hear
beep, beep.

Look!
In the sky!

See it land.
Oh, my!

Oh!
Oh, my!
Out come
space guys.

Mom, Dad,
come see!

Space guys
are in the tree!

Now, now,
go to bed.
Space guys
are in your head.

Oh!

Hi, space guys.

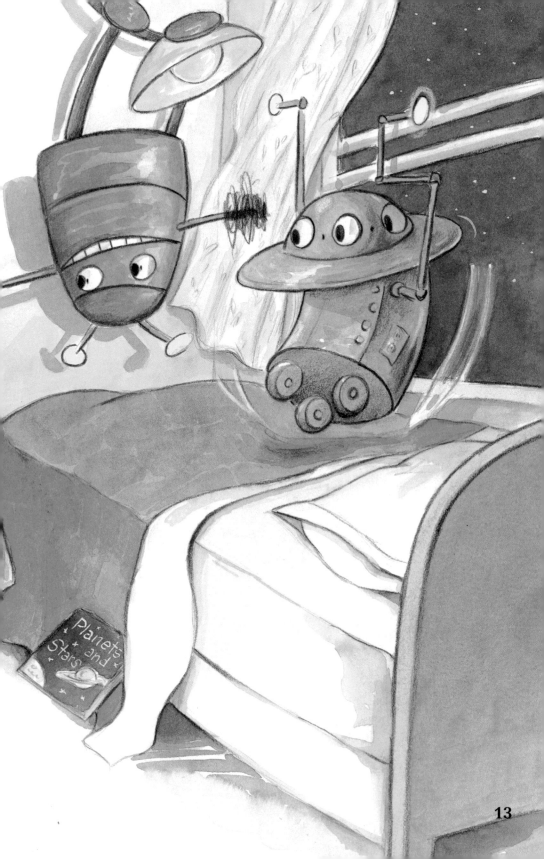

Like my plane?
It can fly.

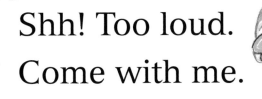

Shh! Too loud.
Come with me.

15

Stop! Don't eat soap!
Oh, no! Yucky!

Not the pot, not the fan.

Eat the pie.

Don't eat the pan!

19

Want to look at the TV?

Here's a show
about a bee.

Space guys! Space guys!
Look at me.

I see you.
Now say "Cheese!"

Time to go?
But not with me.
Don't take Kitty!
Don't take me!

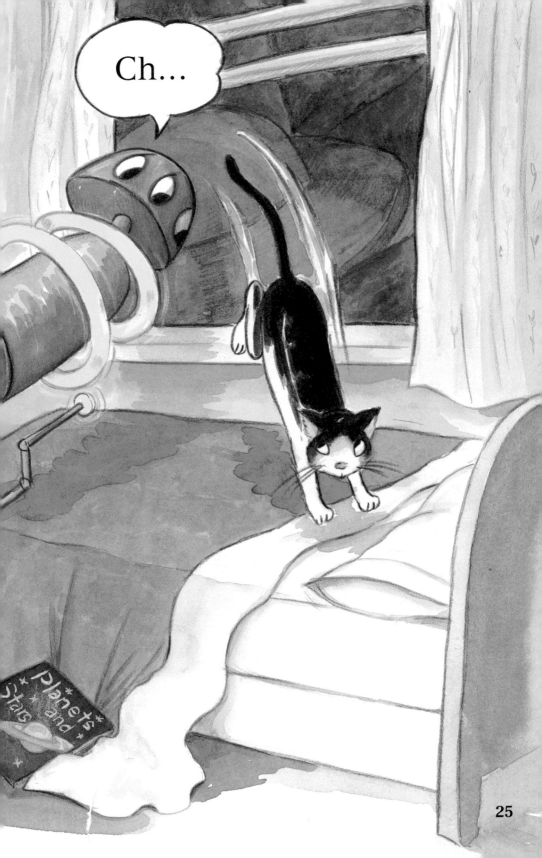

Bye, bye, space guys.
Say hi to the sky.